# SOPHIE'S TIMEPIECE

First published 2008
Evans Brothers Limited
2A Portman Mansions
Chiltern Street
London W1U 6NR

Text copyright © Mary Chapman 2008
© in the illustrations Evans Brothers Ltd 2008

British Library Cataloguing in Publication Data

Chapman, Mary
    Sophie's timepiece. - (Spirals)
    1. Children's stories
    I. Title
    823.9'2 [J]

ISBN-13: 978 0 237 53530 8 (hb)
ISBN-13: 978 0 237 53534 6 (pb)

Printed in China

Editor: Louise John
Design: Robert Walster
Production: Jenny Mulvanny

# SOPHIE'S TIMEPIECE

## Mary Chapman
## and Nigel Baines

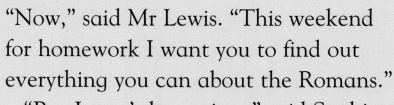

"Now," said Mr Lewis. "This weekend for homework I want you to find out everything you can about the Romans."

"But I won't have time," said Sophie. "My Aunt Rose is coming to stay."

"Well, you'll just have to find time," said Mr Lewis.

But Sophie forgot all about the Romans as soon as she got home.

4

Aunt Rose had arrived, just back
from travelling round the world for
the sixth time!

"I've got a present for you, Sophie,"
she said, handing her a large, round
gold watch.

"Our Great-Grandfather's Timepiece!"
said Mum.

"This is a very special watch, Sophie,"
said Aunt Rose. But she didn't say why.

That night, Sophie dreamed about
Mr Lewis. She really must find
time to do that homework or she'd
be in big trouble on Monday!

Whirr, whirr.

Suddenly, Sophie woke up!

Buzz, buzz.

The room was dark, but the watch was glowing, sparkling, twinkling ... and quivering!

The hands started to spin round and round, faster and faster – backwards!

Then the watch leapt into the air, straight into her pyjama pocket.

The room spun around. Colours and
shapes swirled around her.

She felt so dizzy she shut her eyes.
And when she opened them...

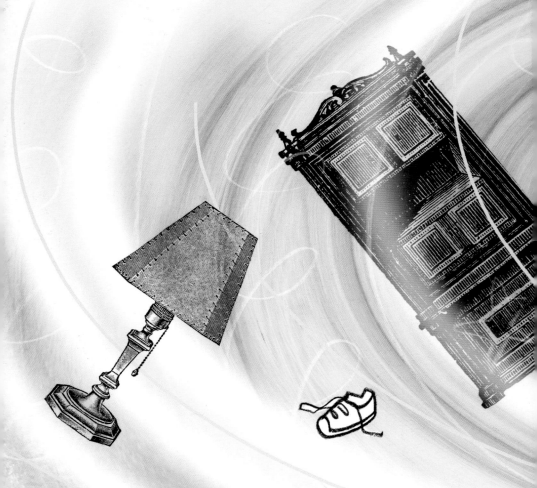

... her room had vanished.

"Where am I?" she asked crossly.

But there was nobody there to answer, except a couple of goats.

"A heap of old ruins!" she grumbled. "Boring! I'm not staying here."

But then...

... the ruins became walls. The walls grew into a town.

Sophie ran down the hill towards a gateway in a high wall.

At the bottom, she peeked in her pocket. The watch was still there.

But the hands had stopped.

There was noise everywhere – men shouting, women laughing, dogs barking, hens clucking, goats bleating, horses neighing. And the smells were nice *and* nasty!

A boy was running after a girl.

"Cornelia!" he yelled.

The girl shouted back, "Flavius!"

She darted through the crowd, laughing.

"I'll follow them,"
thought Sophie.

Sophie ran after Cornelia and Flavius
through the market and down a quiet
street into a courtyard.

But then she lost them.

She looked into a large room off
the courtyard.

"Excuse me," she said.

She coughed. She hummed a little
tune. But nobody took any notice at all.

She stuck out her tongue.

"No one can see or hear me!" she
thought.

But where were Cornelia and Flavius?

She found them in another room.
    "It's a kind of school," she thought,
"but very small. The teacher looks cross.
And I don't like that cane!"

After school the children played games. Flavius grabbed the dice. Cornelia snatched it back.

They began to fight, rolling on the floor, laughing. The other children joined in.

Sophie wished she could, too, but she knew she couldn't. As far as they were concerned she wasn't there.

Sophie walked back to the courtyard.

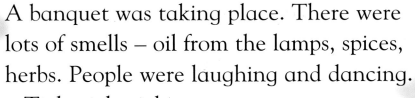

A banquet was taking place. There were
lots of smells – oil from the lamps, spices,
herbs. People were laughing and dancing.

Tick, tick, tick...

Sophie felt the watch in her pocket
quiver. And, once again, shapes and
colours swirled around her...

On Monday at school, Mr Lewis said, "Sophie, this is excellent! It's as if you'd actually visited a real Roman town."

"Yes, I found time to do it after all," said Sophie, smiling to herself.

Why not try reading another **Spirals** book?

**Megan's Tick Tock Rocket** by Andrew Fusek Peters,
Polly Peters and Simona Dimitri
ISBN 978 0237 53348 9 (hb)
ISBN 978 0237 53342 7 (pb)

**Growl!** by Vivian French and Tim Archbold
ISBN 978 0237 53351 9 (hb)
ISBN 978 0237 53345 8 (pb)

**John and the River Monster** by Paul Harrison and
Ian Benfold Haywood
ISBN 978 0237 53350 2 (hb)
ISBN 978 0237 53344 1 (pb)

**Froggy Went a Hopping** by Alan Durant and Sue Mason
ISBN 978 0237 53352 6 (hb)
ISBN 978 0237 53346 5 (pb)

**Amy's Slippers** by Mary Chapman and Simona Dimitri
ISBN 978 0237 53353 3 (hb)
ISBN 978 0237 53347 2 (pb)

**The Flamingo Who Forgot** by Alan Durant and Franco Rivolli
ISBN 978 0237 53349 6 (hb)
ISBN 978 0237 53343 4 (pb)

**Glub!** by Penny Little and Sue Mason
ISBN 978 0237 53462 2 (hb)
ISBN 978 0237 53461 5 (pb)

**The Grumpy Queen** by Valerie Wilding and Simona Sanfilippo
ISBN 978 0237 53460 8 (hb)
ISBN 978 0237 53459 2 (pb)

**Happy** by Mara Bergman and Simona Sanfilippo
ISBN 978 0237 53532 2 (hb)
ISBN 978 0237 53536 0 (pb)

**Sink or Swim** by Dereen Taylor and Marijke van Veldhoven
ISBN 978 0237 53531 5 (hb)
ISBN 978 0237 53535 3 (pb)

**Sophie's Timepiece** by Mary Chapman and Nigel Baines
ISBN 978 0237 53530 8 (hb)
ISBN 978 0237 53534 6 (pb)